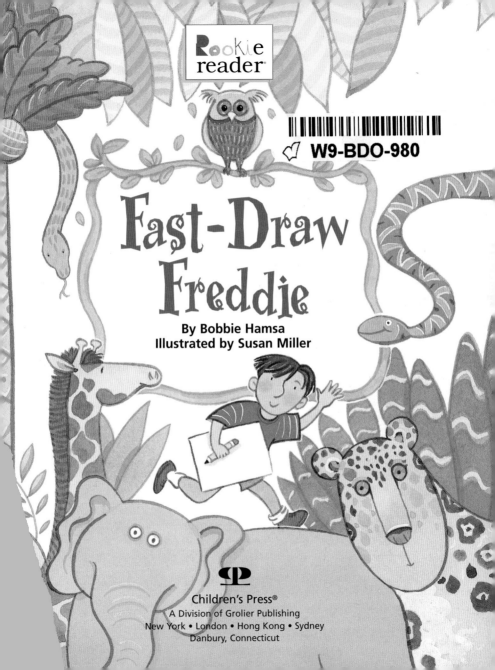

Fast-Draw Freddie

By Bobbie Hamsa
Illustrated by Susan Miller

Children's Press®
A Division of Grolier Publishing
New York • London • Hong Kong • Sydney
Danbury, Connecticut

To Viktor
—S. M.

Reading Consultants
Linda Cornwell
Coordinator of School Quality and Professional Improvement
(Indiana State Teachers Association)

Katharine A. Kane
Education Consultant
(Retired, San Diego County Office of Education
and San Diego State University)

Library of Congress Cataloging-in-Publication Data
Hamsa, Bobbie.
    Fast-draw Freddie / by Bobbie Hamsa ; illustrated by Susan Miller.—Rev. ed.
       p. cm.— (Rookie reader)
    Summary: Freddie draws many different kinds of pictures, including pictures of
Mom, Dad, and Grandma.
    ISBN 0-516-22153-1 (lib.bdg.)   0-516-27150-4 (pbk.)
    [1. Drawing—Fiction. 2. Stories in rhyme.] I. Miller, Susan, ill. II. Title. III. Serie
PZ8.3.H189 Fas 2000
[E]—dc21   99-057170

© 2000 by Children's Press®, a Division of Grolier Publishing Co., Inc.
Illustrations © 2000 by Susan Miller
All rights reserved. Published simultaneously in Canada.
Printed in China.
15 16 17 18 19 R 14 13 12 11
              62

Fast-Draw Freddie
draws pictures fast.

Big pictures.

Rookie
reader®

Fast-Draw
Freddie

By Bobbie Hamsa
Illustrated by Susan Miller

Small pictures.

Short pictures.

Tall pictures.

Thin pictures.

Fat pictures.

Mouse pictures.

Cat pictures.

Pictures of Mom.

Pictures of Dad.

Pictures of Grandma
that aren't too bad.

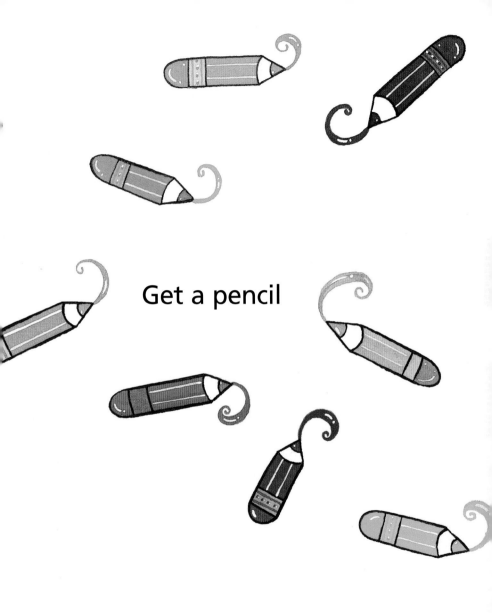

Get a pencil

and a paper or two.

You can be a Fast Draw, too!

Word List (31 words)

a	fast	pictures
and	fat	short
aren't	Freddie	small
bad	get	tall
be	Grandma	that
big	Mom	thin
can	mouse	too
cat	of	two
Dad	or	you
draw	paper	
draws	pencil	

About the Author

Bobbie Hamsa was born and raised in Nebraska and has a Bachelor of Arts Degree in English Literature. She is an advertising copywriter, writing print, radio, and television copy for many accounts. She is also the author of many children's books. Bobbie lives in Omaha with her husband, Dick Sullivan, and children, John, Tracy, and Kenton.

About the Illustrator

Susan Miller has illustrated many picture books. *Fast-Draw Freddie* is her fifth book in the Rookie Reader series. She loves drawing fast in her studio in Terryville, Connecticut, where she lives with her husband, two children, one cat, one dog, and a very fast kitten.

**Read these other Rookie Readers®
at the Early Fluent reading level:**

Sand
Pam Miller

Baby in the House
David F. Marx

Shells
Betsy Franco

Children's Press

U.S. $4.95
Can. $6.95

ISBN 0-516-27150-4

900

9 780516 271507